SILENCER

SILENCER

Marcus Wicker

A MARINER ORIGINAL
MARINER BOOKS
HOUGHTON MIFFLIN HARCOURT
BOSTON NEW YORK
2017

For information about permission to reproduce selections from this book,
write to trade.permissions@hmhco.com or to Permissions, Houghton Mifflin Harcourt
Publishing Company, 3 Park Avenue, 19th Floor, New York, New York 10016.

WWW.HMHCO.COM

Library of Congress Cataloging-in-Publication Data
Names: Wicker, Marcus, author.
Title: Silencer / Marcus Wicker.
Description: Boston : Mariner Books, 2017. | Description based on print version
record and CIP data provided by publisher; resource not viewed. Identifiers:
LCCN 2017014165 (print) | LCCN 2017016611 (ebook) |
ISBN 9781328715586 (ebook) | ISBN 9781328715548 (paperback)
Subjects: | BISAC: POETRY / American / African American. | POETRY /
Inspirational & Religious. | POETRY / American / General. | HISTORY /
Social History. | SOCIAL SCIENCE / Black Studies (Global).
Classification: LCC PS3623.I268 (ebook) | LCC PS3623.I268 A6 2017 (print) |
DDC 811/.6—dc23
LC record available at https://lccn.loc.gov/2017014165

Book design by Mark R. Robinson

PRINTED IN THE UNITED STATES OF AMERICA
DOC 10 9 8 7 6 5 4 3 2 1

"*Silencer* disarms and dazzles with its wisdom and full-throated wit. Wicker's highly anticipated second collection snaps to attention with a soundtrack full of salty swagger and a most skillful use of formal inventions that'll surely knock you out. Here in these pages, sailfish and hummingbirds assert their frenetic movements on a planet simmering with racial tensions, which in turn forms its own kind of bopping and buoyant religion. What a thrill to read these poems that provoke and beg for beauty and song-calling into the darkest of nights."

— Aimee Nezhukumatathil, author of *Lucky Fish*
and poetry editor of *Orion Magazine*

"*Silencer* is an important book of American poetry: wonderfully subtle, wholly original, and subversive. Politics and social realities aside, this is foremost a book that delights in language, how it sounds to the ear and plays to the mind. We have suburban complacency played against hip-hop resistance, Christian prayers uttered in the face of dread violence, real meaning pitted against materialism, and love, in its largest measure, set against ignorance. To say *Silencer* is a tour de force would be an understatement. What a work of true art this is, and what a gift Marcus Wicker has given to us."

— Maurice Manning, author of *One Man's Dark*
and Pulitzer Prize finalist

For all of us

Contents

CUL-DE-SAC PASTORAL

I spend a lot of darkness trying not to give up on being human.

— TIM SEIBLES

*Perhaps you'll think it strange that an invisible man should need light,
desire light, love light.*

— RALPH ELLISON

SILENCER

Silencer to the Heart
While Jogging Through a Park

I shouldn't have to go here
with you: a bandit ties the farmer's dog to a century

oak by the untouched creek. You see human
interest piece, sunny & rounding out the evening news

where I see eclipsed casket. Where I say released he will roam
the same radius. Surely, I don't have to tell you there's a gun

semi-automatic & lodged in the black cherry thicket, but I do
have to tell you about the semi-automatic jail cell clanging

open, not for me, because that's just sound world-making.
I'll say it like this: I don't jog in the park with my blindsides

shaded anymore. Look, here, through the spangled screen
door: there was once a kid, ordinary in every American leisure

except one. I won't name him. You'll look away.
Again: there was too much Shepherd's Pie, a slice of Apple

& one sturdy carving knife. In damp air hung glints
of siren moon, few sirens, sleepy porch lamps blinking on

& an ache for antacids that jogged a man
to the corner store, like puttering wind, then back over

the town's little blacktop hills near the park's edge
where there was a shot streetlight & lots of wheezing

over a bench, & there were three shadows, a pit bull
tied to the bench & a bulge in his gut

that was a bulge in his gut, which
must've looked to one shadow like a box cutter & not

a roll of Tums, & then there are, frankly,
too many black cherry thickets streaked with blood.

Sometimes, I can barely walk
out into daylight wearing a cotton sweatshirt

without trembling. & surely I don't have to
tell you who gets put down, which one walks away.

Conjecture on the Stained-Glass Image of White Christ at Ebenezer Baptist Church

For in the one Spirit we were all baptized into one body—Jews or Greeks, slaves or free—and all were made to drink of one Spirit.
— I CORINTHIANS 12:13

If in his image made am I, then make me a miracle.

Make my shrine a copper faucet leaking everlasting Evian to the masses.

Make this empty water glass a goblet of long-legged French wine.

Make mine a Prince-purple body bag designed by Crown Royal

for tax collectors to spill over & tithe into just before I rise.

If in his image made am I, then make my vessel a pearl Coupe de Ville.

Make mine the body of a 28-year-old black woman

in a blue patterned maxi dress cruising through Hell on Earth, TX

again alive. If in his image made are we, then why

the endless string of effigies?

Why so many mortal blasphemes?

Why crucify me in HD across a scrolling news ticker, tied

to a clothesline of broken necks long as Time?

Is this thing on? Jesus on the ground. Jesus in the margins.

Of hurricane & sea. Jesus of busted levees in chocolate cities.

Jesus of the Middle East (Africa) & crows flying backwards.

Of blood, on the leaves, inside diamond mines, in under-

developed mineral-rich countries. If in your image made are we,

the proliferation of your tie-dyed hippie doppelgänger

makes you easier to daily see. & in this image didn't we make

the godhead, slightly stony, high enough to surf a cloud?

& didn't we leave you there, where, surely paradise or

justice must be meted out? Couldn't we see where water takes

the form of whatever most holds it upright? If then this

is what it's come down to. My faith, in rifle shells.

In Glock 22 magazine sleeves. Isn't it also then how, why,

in a bucket shot full of holes, I've been made to believe?

In My 31st Year

Once you turn 30, it's like they take the heart and soul out of a man — out of a black man — in this country, and you don't wanna fight no more.
— TUPAC SHAKUR

OK, so it's true

that last week I let Andrew,

half in the bag, a little crumpled,

cuff my wrists, then

perhaps, too familiar, wing an arm

around my neck, &

then, he even called me his

boy. Yes, regrettably

I let it happen,

near the butler's pantry

in the dean's peat-green Victorian

with the mansard roof —

a mere eyeshot from

the visiting poet, black

(why'd I tell you that?), &

yes, I could have dug hard

my measured nudge —

could have drummed a song

of scotch & wind from his chest

with one thudding blow, Brother

Pac, were it not for my chronic

misfirings in mixed company.

By which, I mean: me, at those dry-ass parties. & too,

that pesky other thing.

One thing worse than being too

seen, is the not being seen, in profile.

Ellison said something like that at 38.

I say, it is still very much like that.

Which is to say I waited,

until all the peanuts from the gallery

had gone. All the olives, the brie,

the mango chutney co-opted

from proper serving trays & safely

out of range to say, *Are you okay?*

Which, I'll admit, was weak.

Dear Pac, if there's a heaven

for a G, the red Rorschach splotches

of cop-shot bodies you must stomach,

floating toward the kingdom

each sunset. Yes, I know I don't see

what you see. But I read the internet

& history. Stand at rallies, weep

openly. I metabolize rage,

almost all of the time.

You're right.

I should know better

than let an old white man too close

to my throat. That's true.

But Pac, what would you do

for love in southern Indiana?

Maybe not ride or die, but a friend

who compliments your Goodwill tie,

when you miss the memo

about a customary cummerbund?

It's a slippery slope, & I know

I shouldn't let Drew slide.

You throw certain folks a rope

& they turn into cowboys.

Holler if you hear me,

sometimes it's hard to tell

the mozzarella from the brie.

O, say can you see

I'm warring inside? & who am I

even really talking to?

Taking Aim at a Macy's Changing Room Mirror, I Blame Television

No chain link fences leapt in a single bound. No juke
move Nike Commercial, speeding bullet Skittles-hued
　　　Cross Trainers. No brown skin Adonis weaving trails of
industrial Vaseline down a cobblestone street. Heisman-shucking
　　　trash receptacles. Grand Jeté over the little blue recycling
bin, a prism of clouds rising beneath his feet. Nobody all-fucked
　　　in boot cuffs wide enough to cloak court-appointed tethers.
Or slumped over, hoodie-shrouded—*sheepishly scary* according to
　　　one eyewitness. Definitely not going to be your Louis V
Sweat Suit red carpet fashion review, coming at you live from E!
　　　& Fox News outside of the morgue. No chance for
homeboy in the peekaboo boxer shorts. Homeboy with the frozen
　　　wrists. Iced. Homeslice with the paisley, Pretty Flacko Flag
flying by the seat of low-slung denim—no defense
　　　attorney gets to call me *Gang Related*. Tupac
in a mock-leather bomber. No statement taken
　　　from the Clint Eastwood of your particular planned
community, saying he had the right to stand his ground
　　　at the Super Target. Because my flat-billed, fitted cap
cast a *shady* shadow over his shoulder in the checkout line. No, siree.
　　　See, I practice self target practice. There is no sight of me
in my wears. I, bedecked in No-Wrinkle Dockers. Sensible
　　　navy blazer. Barack Obama Tie, Double Consciousness-
knotted. Stock dandelion pinned to the skin of an American
　　　lapel with his head blown off.

In Defense of Ballin' on a Budget

Too many people spend money they haven't earned, to buy things they don't want,
to impress people they don't like.
— WILL SMITH

Damn Will—they've got you sounding mighty
Uncle Phil in these streets. Like the still calling
the Ketel One cheap. How, where we started from
is never done with our undoing. To get the job,
always stay starched, creased to death. Fresher
than the interviewer. Stop acting brand new
like you aren't Slick Rick the Ruler of this particular
gem crow era. Like you didn't whip a leased Jeep
in '89. Nigga, please. The Maybach's in your blind
spot. Go back to that playground in middle-class
West Philly, where you were kicking silly rhymes
trying to king yourself. When rocking a jiggy
blazer, paisley, with a snapback seemed like fun.
To impress upon the self, "I'm someone."

Watch Us Elocute

June 18, 2015

So I'm at this party, right. Low lights, champagne, Michael
Bublé & a gang of loafers I'm forever dancing around

in unduly charged conversations, your favorite
accompanist—Bill Evans behind Miles, ever present

in few strokes—when, into the room walks
this potentially well-meaning Waspy woman *obviously*

from Connecticut-money, boasting an extensive background
in nonprofit arts management. & without much coaxing

from me, really, none at all, she whoops, *Gosh, you're just
so well spoken!* & I'm like, *Duh, Son.* So then we both

clink glasses, drink to whatever that was. Naturally,
not till the next morning & from under a scalding

shower do I shout: *Yes, ma'am. Some of us does talk good!*
to no one in particular but the drain holes. No one

but the off-white tile grout, the loofah's yellow pores.
Because I come from a long braid of dangerous men

who learned to talk their way out of small compartments.
My own Spartan walls lined with their faces—Ellison

& Ellington. Langston, Robeson. Frederick Douglass
above the bench press in the gym, but to no avail—

Without fail, when I'm at the Cross Eyed Cricket
(That's a real diner. It's in Indiana.) & some pimple-

face ginger waiter lingers nervous & doth protest
too much, it's always *Sir, you ever been told you sound like*

Bryant Gumbel? Which is cute. Because he's probably
ten. But then sometimes I sit in his twin's section, & he

once predicted I could do a *really wicked impression*
of Wayne Brady. I know for a fact his name is Jim.

I've got Jim's eighteenth birthday blazed on my bedside
calendar. It reads: Ass whippin'. Twelve a.m.—& like

actually, that woman from the bimonthly
CV-building gala can kick rocks. Because she's old

enough to be my mother, & educated, if only
by her own appraisal, but boy. Dear boys. Sweet

freckled What's-His-Face & Dipshit Jim,
we can still be play friends. Your folks didn't explain

I'd take your trinket praise as teeny blade—
a trillionth micro-aggression, against & beneath

my skin. Little buddies, that sore's on me.
I know what you mean. That I must seem, "safe."

But let's get this straight. Let's call a spade a—
Poor choice of words. Ali, I might not

be. Though, at the very least, a heavyweight
throwback: Nat King Cole singing silky

& subliminal about the unforgettable model
minority. NBC believed Nat & his eloquence

could single-handedly defeat Jim Crow.
Fact: They were wrong. Of this I know

& not because they canceled his show
in '57 after one season, citing insufficient

sponsorship. Or because, in 1948,
the KKK flamed a cross on his LA lawn.

But because yesterday, literally yesterday,
some simple American citizen — throwback

supremacist Straight Outta Birmingham, 1963 —
aimed his .45 & emptied the life from nine

black believers at an AME church in Charleston.
Among them a pastor-senator, an elderly tenor,

beloved librarian, a barber with a business degree
who adored his mom & wrote poems about

the same age as me. I'm sorry. No, friends.
None of us is safe.

Ars Poetica Battle Rhyme for
Really Wannabe Somebodies

I'm not here to make friends!
— AMERICA'S NEXT TOP MODEL CONTESTANT

This is for my Liz Taylor
Literati. Gaudy darlings
Ear-hustling your way into &
through ill-lit poet soirees
all kinds of illegitimate like.
You heard who's a sure thing
for which distinguished
fellowship? The one with the
(not-so) super-secretive
selection panel, & one-percenter
endowment? & who was it
who spotted Mark So & So
canoodling with B. D. Wong
last AWP, over extra wet
martinis, top shelf, twelfth floor
of the Hyatt Regency? I see you
checking your Rolodexes —
Feckless. Y'all some young-
actin' Eddie Murphys to me:
too good at doing impressions
for comfort. Must have fell asleep
dreaming of feature readings
& never woke up. Ol' *really* wannabe-

ass somebodies. Go sit down
somewhere & shed. Quit
stalling, squawking
like a sucker & open up.
Come off it, cousin.
Think your favorite, famous
so & so never feared what he
couldn't yet do? Hmpf—think
you're the first fool with a laptop
to ever arrive at a blank screen
& ask, is this enough?

Prayer on Aladdin's Lamp

Grant me shelter & bread.
Grant me porch ledge, mantel.
Scented candles, bed. Grant me
four walls, a 5-foot fridge & a hall.
& maybe four more walls. Yes.
Four more walls. & a desk. &
a decent laptop, plus pleather
rolling chair. So that I might sit
& write you a poem, Lord.
A psalm praising all you've given:
Air I sing with. Cricket's falsetto.
Buzzing bees & nectar—
how chrysanthemum feels
on the tongue
is what you are to me.
You see what I am doing here.
You see, I am being so sincere,
Sire. Which is sad. Still, grant me
a few free hours each day. Grant me
a Moleskine pad & a ballpoint pen
with some mass. Grant me your gift
of this voice. Pages & pages
of this voice, in a good book
from a loving press. & grant me
a great love, too. Grant a way
to provide for my love. Like,
a tenure-track job

at a small college in the Midwest.
The kind with poems
& papers to read. With hoodies
running in & out of my office.
Deadlines, paychecks, &
an OK 401(k). Grant me
everything, Lord. Not today.
But before 28. Be Bulldozer.
Genie. Let every prayer avalanche
me into dust, blank matter. Debris.
Make me worthy. O Lord, make me me.

Plea to My Jealous Heart

Pray without ceasing.
— SAINT PAUL

What's funny is that you think I can stop praying.
That you think I take existence — blown dandelion
across a philtrum — lightly, as irresponsible
birdsong. As the wren, finch, chickadee & prairie warbler.
As scarlet tanager, indigo bunting, laughing gull, trumpeter
swan. As common sparrows
outside my window canting dervish loops. Sparrows
that court the air & multiply. As all the love
at all times, everywhere, you think I take too much in.
You think I take communion wine for granted. Sometimes
the other wine touches me sweetly & you know it. All
the time you know it. This & how communion wine
indebts me — as the man granted new eyes
on a hiking trip. How, when his boot met wet dune, he felt
the sinking in. & still you think I can stop praying? How
hummingbird? How sailfish? Mother-of-pearl moth, little
dragonfly. Old, faithful greyhound. O elephant herd
in a room of rodents, how you have me! Have me
delirious, haggard — hungrier. To hear you
at all times, if it'll keep you redlining reverently.
That's how I love you best. As stethoscope, not
scalpel. As ever-flickering filament, not
kite-adjoined key. Forgive me, a sinner afraid
of lightning, but when I ask you out, o whistling
tailpipe, you suck air from lungs. I inhale & need you

& you know it. As whisper. As hum. As tradewind
& storm, you show yourself no matter my asking.
& when I ask, o elegant cyclone, you wrench flesh
from bone, bone from hip socket. What's funny is that
tender tendon is the blessing & you know my bird bones.
My blood, you course it. You know my slow capacity
for recovery. What's funny is I feel bad for that
& you think I can stop praying? When my lover locks
our pinkies in a crowded art gallery, I praise the body, praise
every kissable knuckle, every painstakingly etched wave
in a fingerprint, & you think I could take a host for granted
o center of every body? O, all-knowing ebbless red sea
I want to look in your face & live this beautifully always.
O metacarpal, proximal, o distal phalange, all-powerful finger
in a breastplate, touch me light as a feather, please, jog in place.

Confessional Booth with Lines from Heartbreak "Drizzy" Drake, Ending on a Theme from Oddisee

I'll admit it, I'll admit it. I actually listen to chatter
about 65% of the time—a conservative estimate
calculated mid-conversation by dividing the number of
times I feel my cheeks rise, head nod, by the likelihood
that X person is 100% rehearsed or rehashing
a highlight reel to fill the ever-growing silence
between us. I do this not because I'm a nice guy—I am—
but because, behind these light eyes, I might be running
'round *the six*th circle of something *with my woes.*
Yo I'm a real good schmoozer but it kills me inside.
I'm quiet with it, private. Island with it. I suppress it,
go get it & just ride with it. Say word to the poetry fans
who requested this so I ran it back like One Time.
& fuck going online, that ain't part of my day!
Shout out to the whole year I watched likes inch up
on a timeline like grass growing in a time-lapse camera.
I've been envy's green blade, a blue bead of sweat.
The *24-Hour Champagne Diet.* Fine cork & empty
stomach, both. I've been about two or three people,
the normal amount. So *please don't speak to me like I'm that
Drake from four years ago, Girl. I'm on a higher level*
of understanding now. I smile at strangers now, assume
we need it. Yesterday, I lied to Matthew, said I loved
his maroon sock tie. *I stay up late at night thinking*
about intention vs. execution, persecution—

Church—Trinity. & whenever my heart is absent

from my absent-minded actions I say *I'm sorry, Girl.*

I keep a good account of my self. Awkward, dweeby

server dude who works at PG on Franklin Street,

I undertipped you. *Sorry.* Last great love, I hurt you.

Worst behavior. Sorry. I had to take the summer off

to get it right, but now I know. When I let the sin rain

out this way I feel half alive, less than scared to death

that this is the best I'll be before You come & collect

my breath back, *Girl.* It's true: I belong to the world.

Ode to Browsing the Web

Two spiky-haired Russian cats hit kick flips
on a vert ramp. The camera pans to another

pocket of the room where six kids rocking holey
t-shirts etch aerosol lines on warehouse walls

in words I cannot comprehend. All of this,
happening in a time no older than your last

heartbeat. I've been told the internet is
an unholy place—an endless intangible

stumbling ground of false deities,
dogma & loneliness, sad as a pile of shit

in a world without flies. My loneliness exists
in every afterthought. Yesterday, I watched

a neighbor braid intricate waves of cornrows
into her son's tiny head & could have lived

in her focus-wrinkled brow for a living. Today
I think I practice the religion of blinking too much.

Today, I know no neighbor's name & won't
know if I like it or not. O holy streaming screen

of counterculture punks, linger my lit mind
on landing strips—through fog, rain, hail—

without care for time or density. O world
wide web, o viral video, o god of excrement

thought. Befriend me. Be fucking infectious.
Move my eyes from one sight to the next.

Stumped Speech on the Internet

I wager it's the hemlock cocktail of anonymity & the id
    feeding the self's out-of-whack Dr. Frankenstein

complex that spooks me. Not the affable ginger day-trader
    who loses a full house — wife, Chihuahua, kids —

in exactly one hand of online Texas hold'em,
    but the asshat hacker who writes a back door

into the code, so he can eye the poor guy's hole cards.
    The internet's crawling with awful shit, man.

You could sleep-click the wrong link & wander down
    the deep hole of your ultimate undoing, see

something you can't unsee. Like a rainbow
    coalition of cops doing calisthenics around

a six-foot, three-hundred-fifty-pound man,
    choked back into the earth for what

looked a lot, to me, like sport. You could watch
    them watching his tired limbs — seize — watch

him end on a bystander's iPhone. & if you, too,
    happen to be a Cancer, you know

that's the kind of thing that could run one
    into hiding, maybe keep you from being OK.

So while I aggressively oppose going outside
    I am pro that viral video where the gray-

bearded Schnauzer greets his owner—back
    home—after two years abroad in Slovenia.

I love it when the senior dog
    shrieks joy, leaps high into her arms

before swooning in the gravel driveway.
    To be so shockingly happy

your consciousness takes leave,
    then returns, is a thought that's healthy

for my heart. To take a momentary
    breather from this country

is another altogether. I don't know,
    maybe it's actually her

free will that ensnares me so.
    To return—

Close Encounters

I was a real cute kid. Ask anybody. My father
likes to tell a story about a modeling scout

who spotted us out midday shopping
at the Briarwood Mall. Imagine 5-year-old me,

all sailor stripes & junior afro, doing a full pull-up
on the magazine kiosk: Got any Keats? No doubt

something I'd heard watching *Jeopardy!*
with granny, but it mattered not

to the tickled-pink lady. *Oh, you're just soooo
sweet! What a cutie-sweet!* she decreed, handing dad

her flowery card. It wouldn't stop there.
My 10th birthday, whole neighborhood invited,

I strutted down the stairs in a white sports coat
like, Look, folks. In case you're wondering,

I'm the host! My mother told Mrs. Holbrook,
He was born full grown with a briefcase. As I'm sure

you will be, little sewn seed, undone. Future me.
Dear son, the defacing starts much later.

After desegregation sparks the awkward clutch
of Coach clutches on campus buses, but before

the riots in Baltimore. It started a few days before
I turned 30. Invisibility. Home from teaching

the sons & daughters of Indiana farmhands
it's OK to write poems, same briefcase slung

tired across wrinkled linen, you'd have thought
I accosted her—Maria—when I stooped down

to pluck my mother a pair of magenta tulips
from her own thriving garden, & she shrieked,

Why are you looking at my lawn! Maria, who
used to slide teen-me a twenty to occupy her

daughter in the playpen while she grabbed
a bottle of Bordeaux from the basement

before the *real nanny* arrived. She must have seen
straight through me, into the distant past, alternate

reality when your grandparents' neighboring
residence would have been a servants', & I

in that moment, for the first time, unsaw her.
As primer. A kind of manila cardstock

I'd failed to imprint. Son, sometimes this happens.
It happens in gated spaces when you look like

a lock pick. See the 44th president. Scratch that.
It happens in gated spaces, as the lone

locksmith. & if I'm being honest,
the happy way things are going between

me & E., you may well resemble him.
Don't count yourself precious. Truth is,

too soon, you will bend down to rob a few
bright blossoms from your own land &

look away from the earth
to make certain you haven't been ogled.

This phantom guilt applied to a nape
through the eyes of every blind Maria,

here's the key: try not to let it die.
Now run to the closest mirror, quickly

remember how sweet the fleeting love.

Creation Song in Which a Swift Wind Sucker-Punches a Transformer

In which the transformer heaves projectile from the telephone pole.
In which the pole snaps awake — its miter-box guts emptied out
over an oscillating fan. In which atomized rot rains
atop the Crabapple's pet-name pheromones, in which nobody notices.
Creation song in which electrified shrapnel voids:
Bedazzled yard gnome, limestone garden ornaments. Remote control
Ferrari, real-life Range Rover, in which somebody notices.
Creation song in which six kids crowd around pigskin
curious, the tallest boy prodding the ball with a stick.
Creation song in which your online bank account is unavailable.
In which your exquisite 60-inch flat-screen is an HD plastic heap.
In which the matchstick feels Paleolithic & you could be making love.
Creation song in which unattended sparks sizzle along a chain
link fence. In which everyone heads for the gates.

Silencer on the Arrest of Professor Henry Louis Gates Jr. After Sassing an Officer Who Assumed He'd Unlawfully Entered His Own Home

So first you saw this: Pitch, gumming a two
party wagon wheel — mule. Before the cart
   before the cartwheeling wheel. After, mule
suspended in action pose across *Sports*
   Illustrated. See the mule saunter forth:
low smoke oxbowing a manicured maze
   of hedges. When a man is made of ghosts
& soot, broken, stuck in a time loop, he's
   a fixed interloper in at least one
dimension. When a man is a concept
   made of ash & scholarship, ivory
theses, factually sound arguments,
   it's easy to forget he's been granted
a key that sticks. If/then/when he is ground.

Silencer with Blues & Birds on a Wire

My mind is playing tricks on me.
— GETO BOYS

Will you miss the lone, stiff mister bluebird
ghosting it through a two-light town, in which
　you raise your chicks or cocks in Gothic dens
adorned in old doilies, rooster trinkets,
　a sweet aphorism, cross-stitched & hung
above the door? Or maybe you're me-like,
　treading light, an Ave. where birds are called black-
blue—few, but enough for you to notice
　each absence. This deafening black swan song
I hear in wind, wrestling dark pansies
　against headstones—Dixie fifes. It shivers
my spine in sirens nigh, as wince, whiplash
　automatic—yes, bathed in swish of red
& white light, streetlamps crook like Georgia pines.

The Trees

fuck with me.
Something gnarly
    about their medieval acne, something
        a little smallpox in their brown diseased calcified
                        legions, their worry-
ringed folds, so much like the white ball caught in the throat
  of my granddaddy's Negro League catcher's mitt.
                Something in their centuries-old smirk—
        ever watching.   The crow, above a fir,
           circling back.
  Admit it.
They're plain unsettling, you know—
    the whole giant,
        rickety dick motif.
  Not to speak of their slithering hair. Their moptop
of decrepit, other smaller dicks, assaulting the air.   Conveniently,
  ecologists never wager why, every spring,
    droves of frolicking white people, in head-to-toe L.L. Bean,
        seek refuge beneath their leafy hoods.
  Sheeeeeeeit, I wish
a motherfucker would ask me to bike a dirt trail, while some white
    pines circle jerk, ejaculating their replicating,
  mutating microspores,
      their goldenrod
    pollen, into any thing that might sprout
  green.

Blue Faces

after Kendrick Lamar

Never look a gift horse in its nickel-plated grill, lest you've come itching for a lesson in penny stocks. Exhibits A–M: Jordan's heirless, raffled mansion. Jump-shot dreams & white rocks (those, too). Hip hop's hot topics: the Phantom & Maybach. Given the blueblood exclusivity of the oil industry, give us Sprewells. Chrome helicopter wings. Rims that continue to spin stopped short of a destination. Wide enough to bank the sun against crumbling brick party-store walls. Given the blueblood fields, the amber waves of grain, give us all gold everything: gold watch, gold chains, three sparkling pinky rings dropped in Ace of Spades champagne like a garnish. Given the cure for wealth is wealth, give us the generic shit. Why else you think we drink French liqueur & blow through money? No Super PAC for tax-break dairy & coal money. Cashier holding my twenty up to the light to see if it's real money. Like I'd be shopping at Walmart if I could counterfeit money.

Theorizing Wesley:
On the African American Nonresident Alien

as performed by Kendrick Lamar

What you want you a house, you a car? Forty acres & a mule? A piano? A guitar? What you need you a bond, you a tree? Printing press? A receipt? A monopoly piece? America think you crazy, Wesley. Say you black vampire tax cheat suckling the teat. Claim you unfair welfare. Fuck that—America owe you get-back. Three years. Owe you bodies back, dividends from crack. America owe you Reaganomic entitlements redistributed in the form of walk-in closets fat with cream & Sam's Club linen walking suits. America owe you state school–brochure tokenism, the lie of integration. America owe itself acceptance. Owe you Asian & white women. Owe you those OJ & Michael Jackson complexes, respectively. America owe itself therapy in whatever mode you dream fit.

Film Noir at Gallup Park, On the Edge

of suburbia in flux behind one of the town's, count 'em, two
mega high schools. The sometimes-tended-to nature preserve
where green & green slide crisp between brisk handshakes,
where a middle-aged Jimmy John's driver suddenly halts
his '98 Corolla, goes noiseless. Where the sun isn't exactly
booming, but it's Sunday morning & I'm in my feelings,
so I clop off a few paces, nice & easy-like. I mouth hello
to the lovable maintenance man. Hello,
lovable maintenance man I nod. He fusses with his
mustache, flicks it out in a full-tilt wave. In the way
of *mise-en-scène,* I feel compelled to say it's 2014.
I'm a black American poet, newly thirty & middle class
for the Midwest. So far it's the summer of two brothers
unarmed, erased, posterized. Two more & I live
my best days outside like this, under threat
of rain: me, my bad form & no one looking on
with the evil anvil of a hoisted eyebrow. The deceptive flip
of an A-line bob—hand readied to protect the old money
maker. Accordingly, smoke: a slinky Asian teen
makes his body into a nickel, wheels up the wide alley
between me & the trail's opposite edge. Our shades, night-
slick, reflect one another—different frames
from about the same shelf. I catch myself for an instant
in his left lens & wonder was it the Rocky-look
I'm rocking? Was it the bare-bones, bone-white, hooded
Egyptian-cotton track suit drawn tight around my head
like a swim cap? (It's summer here.) Or the ox calves

teetering a chest somewhere between barrel & breasted,

depending on the wind, the Taylor Swift–red grin

of my diabolical office nemesis, or the moon

cycle, maybe anything? Fin—

In the director's cut I'm the one being fatally

femme: I pretend to check my face in the rearview mirror,

pull a plume from a pinner & squeeze the trigger

on a can of lavender Febreze. I chase myself out the window

smarting every time someone flinches at the sight of me.

Metaphorically, I could only be the pitch-dark

asphalt simmering in this parking lot. The fog lifting off

a black tar river, already gone. Though obviously, given

the opportunity, nay the luck—I'd play delivery boy,

even maintenance dude. Anything but walking dead

man. & I'll be damned if I didn't just run

all this way to tell you that. Fuck.

When I'm alone in my room sometimes
I stare at the wall, & in the back of my mind
I hear my conscience call

me Ishmael. Call me sailor. But not
captain. Call me fishhook. Clean.
Call me multipurpose fish scale
weighing self-obsession. Call me fish-
tail in a siren's silk sheets. Thief
in the night. Buccaneer. Call me
multipurpose fish scale singing
motherfucker, then calling it good.
Call me lukewarm algae eater
upchucked. Call me match head struck
against hollow whale walls. Call me
faith's phosphorus irritation. The Bible-
study-leading-Sea-World-trainer-
dead-between-Shamu's-teeth. Call me
Freightliner hull hacking through a baby
humpback. Extinct & extinguished. Son
of a slave girl expelled to the desert
for being himself. Call me
miracle. Opposite mirage. Three parts sea
but bountiful land. Call me mangy
pasture. Wild buffalo. Archer. Arrow.
Call me sheared. Call me back
to the shepherd. Call me lamb.

The Way We Were Made

But you made every
delicate, elegant wrist
& glistening ankle.
But you made them
beautiful
in braided rope
& dime store gold.
But you made every
necklace clasp.
But you made them
caress the nape
like an errant wind
after a shower.
But you made every
eyelash erotic. Every
single strand of hair
soft.
But you made them
from dust & bone.
Made every glorious
singing thigh. Every
button nose.
But you made them
with holes—
wide open
to the faintest hints
of salt

in a sea breeze, salt
in the sweaty mouth
of a navel, salt
in the blood, sweet
in every wrong way.

Incident with Nature, Late

Clean, the gust, prying
me open for the first time
this week—as I—
not exactly wind-
like in the running
thirty & already hunched
over after three stoic
blocks & one big sloppy
knock into the neighbor's
knotty fence decide it
as good a place as any
to stop, pant
& smell the roses—
except there are no
roses, proverbial
or otherwise, except
a nondescript shrub
quivering
with what I hereby dub
the "piney-ness
of an Indiana March"
& oh my God
it feathering my nose
hairs stirring in me
a place where finally
I decide to quit
dicking around

& dig my face in it
low bent, hands cupped
over kneecaps
my eyes adjusting
always for some throbbing:
this sweet bumblebee rushing
through an interstate
of arteries & wishbone
forks in the bush's gut
for a derelict cherry
bloom wearing blush
that hummingbird
in hot pursuit, humming
little drone holy
shit I swivel too late
& she hammers
her needled beak
through my ear drills
hard the run of bone
behind my lobe
& sticks —
All my life, I've been
biblically acquainted
with the donkey-face sting
of avertable night:
usually some small game
slight, some gnat-sized fowl
wedging itself in
where there had always been

light, but just then, momentarily
less—so predictably me
I wave it in, let it pitch a tent
in my living room, bore
heavy-duty stakes through
the Pergo floor, let it crack
walnuts with my violet
mini-stapler, split dishes
with the weight
of peat moss–bricked
lasagna, this lazy ache
I let him knock around inside
my record crates, floss
his beak with the grooves
of my favorite 45
until all I am is a busted song
of nerve tentacles swimming
beneath the pink umbrella
of a redbud tree or all
I am is a singing
saw through a bell
of flesh—the point
being not the ear
but maybe the thorn
is god, little-winged
& hovering here, quietly
in me, when I sit real still
to feel my nature opening
its mouth to speak.

Shibboleth

Say curtsey. Say fold yourself, humble
statue. Say on your knees, Sasquatch-hearted
servant. Say stay there. & think about it, &
say it. Say it via flex, washboard abs
chiseled in your brow. Stand, say it chalice-
jawed: head sky-cocked, eyeballs doused
in stained-glass splendor. Or in your slight sway
say, I come here for the hors d'œuvres, wine. Say
your cowbell is fucking with my inner waltz, fam.
I said it. Here & nowhere else. Say No, I will not
be moved to shudder on command. To flutter even
one finger across the face in the shape of a cross
mid-conversation is crass—parable & prayer, saint.
Don't say that at all. All to say you belong, believer.

When academia tells me only a fool believes in a God that he can't see

I draw them in from a crowded street with a wink
                          & an eye toward the big guy's

wallet.   I sink into myself
                        into my spot   behind the cardboard box

dropped—just here, a prop.   Keep your eyes on the ace
                        of hearts.   Not the ping-ponging pair

of clubs.   Watch
                        the watch.   Just my white gold

watch   not the wrists

                        flickering   windshield wipers

shuffling   gloved hands
                        not this hand–over–hand watch

we keep over one another's

                        peach sunsets   one's palm trees

& green leaves   one's narcotic happiness or
                             holiness   when the heart

of the matter   is the magic
                        is me.

On Being Told Prayer Is a Crutch

So what if it is?
Clear days, I understand it,
molecules scatter azure

light from an in-his-feelings-
sun, & that's why
the sky is blue. We know

too much, or want to.
Not the Bible, but the i-
Phone tells us so.

Devotion doesn't work
that way, but it does. Not
the path, per se, for me

though, a trail back to grace-
fully living with one's light
shone toward higher

axioms than I
can presently see.
It's the immediacy

of a just-thought
thought, thundering
into a device

of my own decided making,
prayer. You know it as *Siri*.
I call it instant intimacy.

Deer Ode, Tangled & Horned

Always the sun first
then the doe sunning, the stag
running toward the doe, wherein

this ramshackle causality
a taste for flesh buds
at birth—when mouth clasps

to breast—quieting
the gut's ache, not hunger
for touch. If you don't believe

touch is a famine
fed by need, in another
scene, see an orphaned fawn

bow before a block of salt
crowned on the lone stump
in a clearing where sudden

wind has instructed him
in a lick's dripping scent.
Right. Now, who then

betrays his permanence
but the huntsman—
himself? Who then but palate—

appetite's kissing cousin, driven
only by science of nature—
O Desire, you mother-

fucker. You Adam
of the valley, crouched
with a catcher's mitt

always signaling for the quince
to roll downhill. You're not much
of a nurturer from behind

this rifle scope,
especially on nights when
I am Lot's hermaphrodite wife—

all pillar
& looking back
on my downfall from the future

which is surely paradise
or purgatory, depending
on how I decipher my scripture, O

Desire, if you're a Catholic's
Tree of Life I must be Buddhist-
free. I'm not interested

in you for the progeny
so much as your skyscraping—
your telephone poles—miraculous,

glazed, glistening with December's
beckoning slick—crisscrossed
with tiny horizontal beams, wired-

horizon & morning dew,
forming, Dear Sire,
your anointing—this

intimately connected rosary
I can't help but prick
my tongue to.

Nocturne with Revelations
& Militant Black Jesus

The world changes. A gradual dusk streaks through
    town & suddenly you're scared to leave the house
without SPF ChapStick or soymilk facial rejuvenator.
    Say black locust night, bog oak-long
shadow, East Indian ebony, Peruvian
    walnut: constellation of dark woods
eclipsing your little girl's heart, & hip hop
    is a motherfucker, ain't it?
I'm talking global get-down.
    Peep — I'm talking de la sol
with correct techniques, slow-draining
    a full-bodied Sauvignon Blanc
on the living room couch, legs scraping
    cathedrals from the sky
above her rim, until one limb & twenty-three
    twigs up the family tree, a perfectly-
Angloed mulatto law pupil finds himself
    behind red velvet night
club rope. Something about inappropriate
    footwear. Keep up. Interest rates
in Des Moines commit hara-kiri
    when lenders see mirrors
in a borrower's brown eyes.
    Then the Beast be a banker's
summer cottage underwater
    for the first time, sí.

Next it goes: double-booked shrinks,
        gun sales, Quaaludes, Fin —

Dear Black Jesus. Dear Morgan Freeman.
        Dear woolen fade of sea-
sick waves. Dear Carlton & bronze sneaks
        beneath a New Orleanian brass band
busking for spring breakers on Frenchman Street.
        In the second coming, pipe your mighty
horns proud, folk! Spread the good news
        until everyone looks like You.
Then, no colonies but those of melanin.
        Then, no hate but the usual
self-loathing. Not one crucified
        with 16 rounds by the Gestapo
always gunning for us & getting away
        because no Gestapo. No black mass
incarceration rate because, no white-masked
        grandparents. No wide masts. No hoods
but neighbors. Just us. All of us left
        with the age-old problem of how best to
love each other.

Ars Poetica

Too late—the path to righteousness gone cold
& everywhere a forked tongue, split road

       dividing line—
toward, away, toward—the divine, unraveling like anise, black
licorice in the night. Psych—Nothing that dramatic. Nothing quite
so unpalatable, destitute, but I did leave the church. I kept
praise, its utterances. I kept guilt, do unto others, & not much else
except You. Please don't worry too much about me. I left

          a window
cracked wide, view enough to see myself back, in case of fire. I've left
frequencies staticky, radios blinking MAYDAY MAYDAY
from a gashed motherland, kept them flickering my veins like angry
lightbulb filaments, left errant, purposely. I try so hard to be good
at mercy. Though, sometimes, a wound is the salve, & besides,
harder to forgive the self when I don't always recognize my flaws
as ill intentioned or otherwise. I'd try You in Taoism, yoga. I've tried
expensive whiskey, tried running suicides. I've tried this one

        blue stone
skipped across a transom, tried the joyous nectar residing between
several varieties of thighs. I'd try anything to sound a shot heart,
my bottomless racket. I'd do anything to live quietly
in You, Father, Maker, Mother, Muse, I try so hard I try. I really do.

The Most Dangerous Game

after Richard Siken

I crack the sliding glass door wide enough for an animal, immortal
                                    to ascend a fleeced deck
    in dying dark. Motion lights keep time with the Bic's rusted flint,
& suddenly the deer stilled against snowcapped pines—
        scavenging what? A few brambles, twigs? Buried buds of ash?
        Hand-me-down cowpeas dappling bird scat? A cul-de-sac's not
                exactly trading up. Of course, the lilac-scented spring.
Sure, summer dogwoods. But often the rabid hound off its tie-out.
                                        Funny thing about
forced migration, always the natives angling your demise. I slide a roach
    from black lips for the neighborhood
                        watch, bow cocked, above his house
in the deer blind. At this height, I'm retreating
        ice pond in a patio table.
                        Spotted face in an antiquated fable.

Animal Farm

Consider the toucan's festive gold breast.
Its multicolored pecker, oddly cutesy
& perhaps, a cartoon-comfort
to the gym-roped westerners
reclining on a beach in Costa Rica.
It's the same old song: good-natured
smile, hard work, a hat's off kind
of attitude & before you can say
postracial, you're a Resort Toucan.
The benefits are room & board
but the cost is blood. Most times
it's the closest ones—birds
of the same rainforest, same
quadrant, same tree—who give up
your whereabouts to the jaguar.
Quick as you got the gig, the boss
is tossing you out on your ass
all over some flipped umbrellas
& a tourist's scarfed thumb. So now
you're roofless, alone, vulnerable
& the beast is licking his chops
in your mirrored aviators. Stifling
too is the Midwestern Subdivision
in its treatment of the black squirrel.
Science tells us black squirrels
have driven out native gray squirrels
in numerous areas, but no bullshit

in my development, black squirrels

are relegated to lots with a view

of the highway. Mornings

they work shade for acorns

between homes narrow as Lincoln Logs.

History tells us black squirrels

can't afford robust landscaping

but will pay their mortgage —

chair the neighborhood watch

if you like. Slenderizing, their night

of hair. They're sun's prey.

They avoid overexposure, make tanning

trend. Black squirrels,

they fit in, get along. Know no one.

They see other black squirrels & run.

CUL-DE-SAC PASTORAL

Ars Poetica Battle Rhyme
for Sucker Emcees

after Adrian Matejka

Who shall not be named.
Who shall not be coveted
beyond whatever
well-mannered Hot 100–
UK List. (You pick.)
Who, keep it real, may not
even exist after this
riff, after this rift. Who,
you may not even claim
ten years from this
line when finally the mic
splits from his mitts—
Check it: anyone can strum
da DUM da DUM (no SHIT)
on a ceremonial lute.
Even a classically trained
orangutan, though
most of you be absolutely
abecedarian. Parakeets:
Dactyls. Basic
Bitches, Simpleton Sarahs
& disco loops. Yo!
you gave up on the moon
for a tweed suit &

elbow patches.
Does your heart also
beat watch-slow,
in perfectly fixed
patterns? Does your stroke
not stroke? Poor you.
Who me?
I be your organic turkey
on steroids. LL—
straight swole, & *hard*
as hell. Bigger. Blacker.
Deafer, you are auto-
tune & I've already
pressed mute.
I be the Anti-wack
ODB. Big Baby Jesus,
Osiris. Bet your wife
might like it. The anti-
virus to your metrics,
flexin'. Got mine honest.
God-given. Got yours, too.

Bay Window Lauds

The sill plays a cruel joke — thrones me. Frames me
lording over lawnmower stripes — myself

in a shallow trench. In grass blades. Myself
persisting, despite a dickhead sun — me

in chlorophyll. Early, I find myself
swaying — me! in the black chokeberry, me!

in the rabbit's throat. Me, the rabbit. Me
dancing-out pellets. Out-dancing myself —

my father's pellet gun, the hawk. The joke
is a bright belly full of dark hopping

along my father's garden & the joke
small, between wrapped talons, is the hawking

too, is the axe sun, swift, rising, this joy.
This joy, it swallows itself far too soon!

Weekend Open House Sext

This joy, it swallows itself far too soon
inside bright balloons, inside banquet tents

inside condiments, inside domestic
beer bottles, inside castled merriment

inside plastic champagne flutes raised skyward
for the neighbor's teen daughter, for he tents

his head, stakes it to the ground, every time
I wave. Help me—For his princess, he tents

her head when I'm inside my SUV
Kangol angled dangerous, so cleanly

cocked. For that, I should show the grad a mouth
of pearly. Merci, Neighbor. For your clean

cul-de-sac-arched mouth clamped, you Clampett.
(—) That. I should surely introduce myself.

Tiki Torch Cookout Vespers

That I should surely introduce myself
to the grill is important. For our guests.

Dear Broil King Master 490, found
you in *Consumer Reports* on my own

then pitched you to Lisa. Love your 3 racks,
ignition switch & spinning spit. Our guests

seem to love you too, especially Pete
with his wandering green eyes. But I own

your stainless steel vessel, your whoop-ticket
double burner system. That we are guests

here — your heat just reminded me. To stop
& smell the butterfly pork chops. We own:

deck, stained fence, city squirrel piss scent, not
you, god in Pete's eyes. You are flammable.

Trash Night Compline

You, god in Pete's eyes, you are flammable
tender. My eyes are a faithful tender

yellow streetlight but this is the tinder
talking now. The nest—twigged, thorned, flammable—

& the ruffled black bird wants to know: What's up
with the burbs, its chemical lawns, tender-

skinned children, its Uzi sprinkler heads? Down
the bowstring power lines blotting tender

twilight—it's the only way I'll leave. Flame
Buicks & midlife crisis sports bikes. Cleanse

this night. O, god in my eyes, you will flame
this cul-de-sac of plastic trash bins, cleanse

these driveways, & if I enjoy & am
the view, Lord, can I still sit next to you?

Materialist Matins

The view, Lord, can I still sit next to you
if it's obscured by an ark's clumsy dark

cloaked in pitch & I am all of it, Sire,
three of every shrine? Ragtop triple black

Cadillac, plus the lease (which is the leash).
Golden calf swung low from Cuban Links. Dark

idolatry: the boardroom brogues buffed just
brighter than the CEO's. Keep these black

as dusk in me where I'll till history
until delinquent cotton blessings, black

gold flowing backwards, & Whig tax codes work
for me, too. Make me visible as you

in Birkenstocks. With Hells Angels Hair. Dark
as slavery: black magic-almighty.

Prayer on the Subdivision

Then I graduate to a four-digit mortgage inside an ornate gate. Me
& two more mes: patent attorney & career soldier. A trinity of clean-
ass SUVs parked beside matching beige tri-levels—proof we own
at least 1/3 the Dream, though my Range is only leased. The tender
kin who invented that adage about good fences must have been black

& living in a cul-de-sac trying to mend an unbreachable wall, black
as light stoking an infrared grill—visible as me
& my family braising grass-fed ribs in Guinness until tender
enough to heal an ulcer. Now that's clean—
Anyway, last spring I host an open house for my niece, figuring I own

the deed, so I can play Frankie Beverly's treatise on loving his own
way loud as I damn well please. Folk slow dancing on a black-
top patio. Auntie Becky louder than the lot of us. D finally clean.
These few, far-between carrots that keep us trotting. The other mes
are curiously unseen despite formal invites & my knocking, tender

as a Girl Scout cookie vendor. & I get it. This tinder
situation, guilt by association at the homeowners'
meeting where I am cited, promptly. Me & only me.
Never mind the Weinsteins' catered blowout where the black
guy gets a knock for weed from their coy teen with the powder-clean

philtrum at an unholy hour. Father, please. Let me stunt, clean
as a Gillette jawline on a solo hunting trip. I'll be a kind of tender-
skinned privilege. A four-sided mirror. Be my own
constitution if living well pleases you. I'd sell my vacation, black
market style, for tithe money even. But, please. Don't make me

do it all in Carlton Banks Argyle. I don't want to be a clean
cut member of any club where I can't rock linen loose enough to
let my junk breathe. Because, after all, Father, you made me.

Conjecture on the Dream

The danger in consuming the Grey Poupon is believing
that you, too, can be a first-generation member of the elite,
turning your nose up at soul music, simple joy, fried foods,
casual Fridays — essentially everything I'm made of. But because
it feels mischievous I sometimes indulge the Dream. Pretend
as if I'm one of the gang, given over to rigorously lazy readings
of Foucault, Foster Wallace, or whoever-the-fuck, because
being true only to the concerns of my own choosing could prove
to be a welcome luxury. Because I'll always favor the mirage
to a mouth, booted-in by spurs, I've been thinking about
installing an infinity pool. Or a Vera Wang mattress set, filled
with professionally chilled Fiji water, so as to be baptized
in palpable comfort. This might be a good time to mention
history's the reason I never learned to swim. What's the use
in playing it like everything's going to be OK for me
in the event of mortal catastrophe, given centuries of thriving
pirate ships, & the state of Louisiana's seventy-odd
hermetically sealed plantations? Given all those gift shops,
I consider myself a renter in this nation of inordinate want.
& what's want but a failed flotation device in a 150-year-old
economic rut? Is it why, after all these lines, I'm afraid
to look you dead in the eye & say, I desire badly
the belly of a bay window storage hatch & chevron-
patterned throw pillows? Why I've got a pocketful of gold
ampersand thumbtacks? A thimble of what may, in fact,
be a caviar fork? Is desire why I'm so terrified of dying
poorly? Why each morning I recite this fleeting prayer
without irony?: Please allow me simply to keep wanting.

Morning in the Burbs

But God, I love the cul-de-sac
at seven a.m., I can't help it!
This wind-streaming-between-
grass-blades point of view!

But this punctuated lawn
I stand upon! The family
of shrubs, flat-topped & shaped
into a question mark:

the eye of its mouth, my favorite
standing place. A painter's steel
scaffold: against the neighbor's
gutter like a concert glockenspiel.

The souped-up air conditioning:
    in monk octaves. The sheer
wash of it all, water rushing
from a bucket: A man soaping

down his Saab, tie sly tucked.
Two cable guys sharing a joint
in a horseshoe drive: But God,
I envy their temporary sweet spot:

snippet of carefree chummery.
This mum machine hard at work
before work. The: The nothing
getting in. The nothing getting out:

Acknowledgments

Grateful acknowledgment is made to the editors of the publications in which the following poems, some in alternate versions, first appeared:

Academy of American Poets Poem-a-Day: "Close Encounters," "Deer Ode, Tangled & Horned."

American Poetry Review: "Plea to My Jealous Heart," "Prayer on Aladdin's Lamp."

Boston Review: "In My 31st Year," "Watch Us Elocute."

Cincinnati Review: "Morning in the Burbs," "Tiki Torch Cookout Vespers."

Iowa Review: "Silencer on the Arrest of Professor Henry Louis Gates Jr. After Sassing an Officer Who Assumed He'd Unlawfully Entered His Own Home."

The Journal: "Creation Song in Which a Swift Wind Sucker-Punches a Transformer," "Shibboleth."

jubilat: "Ars Poetica Battle Rhyme for Sucker Emcees," "Materialist Matins."

Kenyon Review: "Silencer with Blues & Birds on a Wire."

Laurel Review: "On Being Told Prayer Is a Crutch."

Narrative: "In Defense of Ballin' on a Budget," "Incident with Nature, Late," "Prayer on the Subdivision."

Nashville Review: "The Most Dangerous Game."

The Nation: "Film Noir at Gallup Park, On the Edge."

Ninth Letter: "When I'm alone in my room sometimes I stare at the wall, & in the back of my mind I hear my conscience call."

Oxford American: "Silencer to the Heart While Jogging Through a Park."

Paris American: "Weekend Open House Sext."

Poetry: "Animal Farm," "Bay Window Lauds," "Conjecture on the Stained-Glass Image of White Christ at Ebenezer Baptist Church," "Ode to Browsing the Web," "Taking Aim at a Macy's Changing Room Mirror, I Blame Television," "The Way We Were Made."

Public Pool: "Ars Poetica Battle Rhyme for *Really* Wannabe Somebodies."

Third Coast: "Trash Night Compline."

32 Poems: "When academia tells me only a fool believes in a God that he can't see."

"When I'm alone in my room sometimes I stare at the wall, & in the back of my mind I hear my conscience call" appears in *The BreakBeat Poets: New American Poetry in the Age of Hip-Hop* (Haymarket Books, 2015).

"Ode to Browsing the Web" appears in *Literature for Composition* (Pearson, 2016).

"Watch Us Elocute" appears in *Poems for Political Disaster* (Boston Review, 2017).

For notes on *Silencer,* please visit marcuswicker.com.

Endless gratitude to the many, many eyes and minds that loved on this book. Thanks especially to francine harris, Ron Mitchell, Matthew Graham, Adrian Matejka, Ryan Teitman, Keith Leonard, Rebecca Gayle Howell, Jacob Shores-Arguello, Phillip B. Williams, Alexander Weinstein, Cate Lycurgus, Greg Leach, Maurice Manning, Ada Limon, Aimee Nezhukumatathil, and Shane McCrae. Big thanks to Jenny Xu, Editor Extraordinaire, for believing in *Silencer* sincerely and pouring so much energy into its creation. Thanks to the Field Office agency.

To the Fine Arts Work Center, where *Silencer* began, before it was *Silencer,* and to all the fam I made there—immeasurable gratitude. You're all over this book.

Thanks to the Anderson Center, where I penned the book's final poems, and to the May Class of 2016.

To Emily, dearest heart, thank you.

To Mom, Dad, and Brian: Everything I write is because of and for you. Thanks, always.